W9-BHF-056

In Their Shoes

Fairy Tales and Folktales

In Their Shoes

Selected by Julia Nicholson and Anne-Laure Mercier

Illustrated by LUCIE ARNOUX

PUSHKIN CHILDREN'S BOOKS

Pushkin Children's Books
71–75 Shelton Street
London WC2H 9JQ

In Their Shoes: Fairy Tales and Folktales first
published by Pushkin Press in 2015

'The Story of Yexian', published in *Chinese Chronicles of the
Strange: The 'Nuogao ji'* by Duan Chengshi, translated from
the Classical Chinese by Carrie E. Reed, 2001. Reprinted by
kind permission of Peter Lang Publishing, Inc., New York

'Puss in Boots' and 'Hop o' my Thumb' from *The Complete Fairy Tales*
translated from the French by Christopher Betts (2009), pp. 115–126,
151–166. Reprinted by permission of Oxford University Press

'The Story of Chernushka' translation © Julia Nicholson,
2015, translated from the Russian with help from
Clare Fanthorpe and Remi Oriogun-Williams

'Perseus and the Winged Sandals' first published in French in
Le Feuilleton d'Hermès © Éditions Bayard 2006. Translation © Mika
Provata 2014. This translation was first published by Pushkin Children's
Books as part of *The Adventures of Hermes, God of Thieves* in 2014

'The Pair of Shoes' original text © Éditions de La Table
Ronde, Paris, 1967. Translation © Sophie Lewis 2013. This
translation was first published by Pushkin Children's Books
as part of *The Good Little Devil and Other Tales* in 2013

Illustrations © Lucie Arnoux 2015

001

ISBN 978 1 782691 01 3

Text designed and typeset by Tetragon, London
Printed and bound by CPI Group (UK) Ltd, Croydon CRO 4YY

www.pushkinpress.com

Contents

"You never really know a man until you stand in his shoes and walk around in them"

TO KILL A MOCKINGBIRD

The Story of Yexian

of Yexian

DUAN CHENGSHI

THERE IS A STORY AMONG SOUTHERNERS THAT before the Qin and the Han there was a cave master named Wu. The local people called the place Wu cave. Wu took two wives but one wife died, leaving a daughter named Yexian. When she was young, she was intelligent and skilled at metalworking. Her father loved her, but before a year had passed, her father also died. She was treated badly by her step-mother, who often ordered her to collect firewood from dangerous places and to draw water from the deeps.

Once Yexian caught a fish about two inches long with red fins and golden eyes. She placed it in a basin of water. She changed the basin several times, and it grew bigger by the day. Finally it got so big she couldn't find a container for it, and she threw it into the pond in the back. When the girl had leftover food, she would sink it into the water to feed the fish. Whenever the girl came to the pond, the fish would

stick its head out and pillow it on the bank, but it wouldn't do this when other people came. Her stepmother knew about this, but whenever she watched for it, it never showed itself. So she tricked Yexian, saying, "You have certainly worked hard. I'm going to give you some new clothes." The girl changed out of her old clothes. Later the stepmother sent her to fetch water from another spring. Reckoning that the spring was several hundred *li* away, the stepmother slowly dressed in the girl's old clothes, put a long knife in her sleeve, and went to the pond to call the fish. The fish immediately stuck out its head, whereupon she chopped it off and killed the fish. It had already grown to be more than ten feet long. She served its meat, and the taste was twice as good as ordinary fish. Then she hid the bones under the dung heap.

On the following day the girl came back to the pond, and when the fish didn't appear, she went out to the countryside to wail with grief. Suddenly out of the sky appeared a person with loose hair hanging down and wearing coarse clothing. He comforted the girl, saying, "Don't cry. Your stepmother has killed the fish, but its bones are under the dung heap. Now you go back home and hide the bones in your room. Whenever you need something, you have but to pray to the bones and your wish will be granted." The girl did as he said, and gold, pearls, clothing and food came to her as she wished.

On the day of the cave festival the stepmother went out and ordered the girl to keep watch over the fruit trees in the garden. Yexian waited until her stepmother had gone a long way; then she also went out, dressed in a robe spun of kingfisher blue, and wearing shoes of gold upon her feet. The daughter of the stepmother recognized her and said to her mother, "That person looks just like my stepsister." The stepmother also suspected this. Yexian became aware that she had been discovered and hurriedly went back home. On the way she left behind one shoe, which was picked up by a cave dweller. When the stepmother returned home, she only saw the girl fast asleep in the garden, arms wrapped around a tree, so she didn't worry any more about it.

The cave was near an island in the sea. On this island was the kingdom of Tohan. It had a strong army and had sovereignty over dozens of islands.

Its watery coastline stretched for several thousand *li*. The cave dweller sold the girl's shoe in Tohan, and the king acquired it. He told those around him to try it on, but it was an inch too small, even for those with small feet. Then he ordered every woman in his kingdom to try it on, but in the end there was not one person that it fit. It was as light as down, and even when treading on stone, it made no sound. The king of Tohan suspected that the cave dweller had got the shoe in some improper way, so he imprisoned and tortured him, but he never did end up finding out where it had come from. After that, the king threw the shoe down by the wayside, and went through houses everywhere to arrest people. If there was a woman who could wear it, the king's men were to take her into custody and inform the king.

The Tohan king then found Yexian. He ordered her to put on the shoe; then he believed that it was the girl he had sought. Yexian then dressed in her robe spun of kingfisher blue and her golden shoes and went to the king, as lovely as an angel. She began to serve the king as wife, and he took the fish bones along with Yexian back to his country. Her stepmother and sister were killed by flying stones, but the cave dwellers took pity on them and buried them in a stone pit, calling it the "distressed woman's tomb". The cave people did matchmaking sacrifices at this tomb; if they prayed for a woman there, the wish would certainly come true.

When the king of Tohan got back to his country, he made Yexian his primary wife. The first year he greedily prayed to the fish bones and acquired unlimited jewels and jade. The next year the bones simply didn't respond, so the king buried them by the seashore and covered them over with one hundred bushels of pearls, bordering them with gold. Later, when some conscripted soldiers mutinied, their general opened the hiding place to provide for the army. One night the bones were washed away by the tide.

My long-time household servant, Li Shiyuan, told me this story. Shiyuan originally was a Yangzhou cave dweller, and he remembers many strange occurrences of the south.

This is the earliest version of the Cinderella story that has ever been recorded... and it dates back to the 9th century in China. DUAN CHENGSHI was a chronicler and a scholar who lived during the Tang dynasty. He was very curious and travelled a lot. His version of Cinderella is set on the coast of today's Vietnam and was written on a scroll in Classical Chinese.

Puss
in Boots

CHARLES PERRAULT

A MILLER WHO HAD THREE CHILDREN LEFT NOTHing for them to inherit, except for the mill, a donkey, and a cat. These bequests did not take long to share out, and neither the solicitor nor the notary were called in: their fees would soon have eaten up the whole of the miserable inheritance. The eldest son got the mill, the middle one the donkey, and the youngest got only the cat. The young man was inconsolable at being left so meagre a bequest. "My brothers," he said, "will be able to make a decent living if they work together; but as for me, once I've eaten my cat and made his fur into a muff to keep my hands warm, I shall just have to starve to death."

The cat, who could understand what he said, but pretended not to, said in a calm and serious manner: "You mustn't be upset, Master; all you need to do is give me a bag, and have a pair of boots made for me to walk among the brambles, and you will see that you are not as badly provided for as you believe." The cat's master did not expect much to come of this, but he had seen the cat play so many cunning tricks when catching rats and mice, such as to play dead by hanging upside down by his feet or burying himself in flour, that he had some hope that the cat might help him in his wretched plight. When the cat had been given what he had asked for, he dressed up smartly in his boots and, putting the bag round his neck, he took hold of the tie-strings in his two front paws. Then he set off for a warren where there were plenty of rabbits. In his bag he put bran and sow-thistles, and then waited, stretching himself out as if he were dead, for some young rabbit, still ignorant of this world's trickery, to come and poke its nose into it in order to eat the food he had put there. Scarcely had he lain down than he got what he wanted: a silly young rabbit went into the bag, and instantly Master Cat, pulling the strings tight, caught and killed it without mercy.

Full of pride at his catch, he went to visit the King in his palace, and asked to speak to him. He was shown up to His Majesty's apartments, where he entered and said, bowing low before the King: "Sire,

I have here a rabbit from a warren, which My Lord the Marquis of Carabas" (this was the name which he saw fit to give his master) "has commanded me to present to you on his behalf."

"Tell your master," said the King, "that I thank him, and that I am well pleased."

On another occasion, he went into a cornfield and hid himself, holding his bag open again; two partridges went into it, he pulled the string tight, and caught the pair of them. Then he went to present them to the King, as he had with the rabbit. The King was again pleased to accept the two partridges, and tipped him some money. The cat continued in this way for two or three months, from time to time taking game from his master's hunting-grounds to the King.

One day, he found out that the King would be going for a drive along the river in his coach, with his daughter, the most beautiful princess in the world, and he said to his master: "If you follow my advice, your fortune will be made. All you have to do is to go bathing in the river, at a place that I will show you, and then leave everything to me." The Marquis of Carabas did as his cat suggested, not knowing what his purpose was. While he was bathing, the King passed by, and the cat began to shout at the top of his voice: "Help! help! My Lord the Marquis of Carabas is drowning down here!" At his cries, the King put his head to the window, and recognizing the cat who had so often brought him game, he ordered his guards to hurry to the rescue of His Lordship the Marquis of Carabas.

While they were getting the poor Marquis out of the river, the cat went up to the coach, and told the King that, while his master was bathing, some thieves had come and stolen his clothes, even though he had shouted "Stop thief!" as loud as he could (the cat, the rascal, had hidden them under a large stone). The King at once ordered the Gentlemen of the Royal Wardrobe to go and fetch one of his finest suits for His Lordship the Marquis of Carabas. The King treated him with great kindness, and since the fine clothes which he had just been given added to his good looks (for he was handsome and well-built), the King's daughter found him much to her liking. The Marquis had only to throw a glance at her two or three times with great respect and a little tenderness for her to fall madly in love with him. The King invited him to get into the coach and join them on their outing.

The cat, delighted to see that his plan was beginning to succeed, went on ahead, and having met some labourers with scythes cutting grass in a meadow he said to them: "*Good people mowing the grass: unless you tell the King that His Lordship, the Marquis of Carabas, is the owner of this meadow you are mowing, you will all be chopped up, as fine as sausagemeat.*"

The King did not fail to ask the peasants who owned the meadow they were cutting. "It belongs to His Lordship the Marquis of Carabas," they said with one voice, for they were scared by the threat that the cat had made.

"It's a fine estate you have here,' said the King to the Marquis of Carabas. "Indeed, Sire," answered the Marquis, "and that meadow produces an abundant crop every year."

Master Cat, still going on ahead, met some labourers harvesting, and said to them: "*Good people harvesting the corn: unless you tell the King that His Lordship, the Marquis of Carabas, is the owner of all these cornfields, you will all be chopped up, as fine as sausagemeat.*"

The King came past a moment later, and asked who owned all the cornfields he could see. "His Lordship the Marquis of Carabas," replied the harvesters, and the King again congratulated the Marquis. Master Cat, still going ahead of the coach, said the same thing to everyone he met, and the King was astonished to see how much land was owned by His Lordship the Marquis of Carabas.

Eventually, Master Cat arrived at a fine castle owned by an ogre, who was as rich as could be, because all the lands that the King had passed through were part of the castle estate. The cat, who had taken care to find out who this ogre was, and what he had the power to do, asked to speak to him, saying that he did not like to pass so near his castle without having the honour of paying his respects. The Ogre received him as politely as an ogre is able to, asking him if he would like to rest a while.

"I have been told," said the cat, "that you have the gift of turning yourself into all kinds of animals, for instance, that you could change into a lion or an elephant."

"That's quite true," replied the Ogre roughly, "and to prove it, watch me turn into a lion." The cat

was so scared to see a lion standing before him that immediately he sprang up on the roof, which was quite difficult and dangerous because of his boots, which were no good for climbing over tiles. Some time later, seeing that the Ogre had gone back to his original shape, the cat came down, admitting that he had been really frightened. "I have also been told," he said, "but I can scarcely believe it, that you also have the power of taking the shape of tiny little animals, for instance of turning into a rat or a mouse, but I must confess that I think it quite impossible."

"Impossible?" retorted the Ogre; "just wait and see"; and in a moment he changed himself into a mouse, which began to run about the floor. No sooner had the cat seen it than he jumped on it and ate it up.

Meanwhile the King had seen the Ogre's fine castle as he went by, and thought that he would like to go inside. The cat, hearing the noise made by the coach as it passed over the drawbridge, ran to meet it, and said to the King: "Welcome, Your Majesty, to the castle of His Lordship the Marquis of Carabas."

"My goodness, Marquis!" exclaimed the King, "is this castle yours as well? – I can't imagine anything finer than this courtyard with all its buildings around it. Let us see what is inside, please."

The Marquis offered his hand to the young Princess, and following the King, who went first, they entered a great hall, where they found a magnificent banquet. The Ogre had had it set out for his friends, who should have been coming to see him on that very day, but, because they knew the King was there, dared not come in.

The King, delighted by the good qualities of His Lordship the Marquis of Carabas, just like his daughter, who loved him to distraction, said to the Marquis, seeing the great riches that he possessed, and after he had drunk five or six glasses of wine: "If you want to be my son-in-law, my Lord Marquis, you have only to say the word." The Marquis bowed deeply, and accepted the honour that the King had done him; and that very day he married the Princess. The cat became a great lord, and never chased a mouse again, except to please himself.

The Moral of this Tale

Although the benefits are great
For one who owns a large estate
Because he is his father's son,
Young men, when all is said and done,
Will find sharp wits and commonsense
Worth more than an inheritance.

Another Moral

If the son of a miller, in ten minutes or less,
Can take a girl's fancy, and make a princess
Look longingly at him, it proves an old truth:
That elegant clothes on a good-looking youth
Can play a distinctly significant part
In winning the love of a feminine heart.

Puss in Boots is a French and Italian fairy tale from the Middle Ages. The earliest known writer of this story is Giovanni Francesco Straparola, but CHARLES PERRAULT – who lived in France in the 17th century – is the first one who recorded the famous version that people are so familiar with today.

Hop o' my Thumb

CHARLES PERRAULT

ONCE UPON A TIME THERE LIVED A WOODCUTTER
and his wife, who had seven children, all of them
boys. The eldest was only ten years old, the youngest only seven. You may find it surprising that the
woodcutter had so many children in so short a time;
but the fact is that his wife was a quick worker, and
never produced fewer than two at once.

They were very poor, and the seven children
were a great burden, since none of them was old
enough to earn his living. What grieved them even
more was that their youngest son was very delicate,
and hardly ever spoke a word, which they took to
show his stupidity, although it was a sign of intel-
ligence. He was very small; when he was born he
was hardly bigger than a man's thumb, for which
reason Hop o' my Thumb was what he was called.
The poor child was the family scapegoat and was
always given the blame for everything. Despite this,
he was the cleverest of all the brothers, and had the

33

sharpest wits, and though he did not say much, he listened a lot.

There came a year when times were very hard, and the shortage of food was so severe that the wretched couple resolved to get rid of their children. One night, after the children had gone to bed, while the woodcutter was sitting beside the fire with his wife, he said, with despair gripping his heart: "As you can see, we no longer have enough food for the children; I cannot bear to see them dying of hunger before my eyes, and I have decided to take them with me into the wood tomorrow and leave them there to get lost, which will be easy enough; for while they are occupied collecting sticks for firewood, all we will have to do is run away without letting them see."

"Alas!" said the woodcutter's wife, "how could you take your own children away in order to get rid of them?" However many times her husband told her how poor they were, she could not agree to his plan: she was poor, but she was their mother. Nonetheless, after reflecting on the pain it would cause him to watch them dying of hunger, she did agree, and went to bed in tears.

Hop o' my Thumb had overheard everything they said, because he could tell from his bed that they were discussing family business, and he had quietly got up and hidden under his father's stool, so as to be able to listen without being seen. He went back to bed and stayed awake throughout the rest of the night, thinking of what he would have to do. He rose early and went down to the edge of a stream, where he filled his pockets with little white pebbles, and came back to the house.

They set off, and Hop o' my Thumb kept quiet, saying nothing to his brothers of what he knew. They went into the deepest part of the forest, where none of them could see the others even from ten paces away. The woodcutter began cutting trees, and the children to gather twigs for making bundles of firewood. Their father and mother, seeing them busily at work, gradually went further away, and then suddenly ran off, along a hidden path.

When the children saw that they were alone, they started to cry and shout as loudly as they could. Hop o' my Thumb let them cry, since he was certain that he would be able to find his way back to their house; while they had been walking along the path, he had dropped the little white pebbles he had in his pockets. He told them, therefore: "Brothers, never fear; our father and mother have left us here, but I will show you the way back to the house; just follow me." They followed him, and he led them towards the house by the same path that they had taken through the forest. They did not dare go in at once, but pressed themselves against the door to listen to what their parents were saying.

Just at the time when the woodcutter and his wife were returning home, the lord of the manor had sent them ten silver crowns which had been owing to them for a long time, and which they had given up hope of ever seeing again. It saved their lives, for the wretched couple were dying of hunger. The woodcutter sent his wife out straight away to the butcher's, and because it was a long time since they had had anything to eat she bought three times as much meat as she needed for supper for the two of them.

When they had eaten their fill, the woodcutter's wife said: "Alas! where are our poor children now? All these leftovers would make a good meal for them. And, William, it was you who wanted to get them lost; I told you we would regret it. What will they be doing now in that forest? Alas and alack! perhaps they have already been eaten by the wolves! It is very cruel of you to abandon your children." The woodcutter eventually grew impatient, as she repeated a score of times that they would regret it and that she had told him so. If she did not hold her tongue, he said, he would give her a beating. Not that he himself was not upset, perhaps even more than his wife, but rather that she gave him no peace, and he resembled many other men in being very fond of women who speak well, while finding those who have always been right very troublesome.

The wife was all in tears, crying: "Alas! where are my children now, my poor children?" Then once she said it so loudly that the children outside the door heard her, and started to shout all together: "Here we are! here we are!" She ran quickly to let them in, and said, as she kissed them: "How happy I am to see you, my dear children! How tired you must be, and how hungry! Peter dear, you're all covered in mud, come and let me clean you up." This Peter was her eldest son, whom she loved more than any of the others because his hair was reddish, and hers was as well. They all sat down to table, and ate with such an appetite that it did their parents' hearts good to see them, and the children all talked at once almost all the time as they told them how frightened they had been in the forest.

The good people were full of joy to see their children again, and their joy lasted as long as the silver crowns; but when the money ran out, they fell back into their former despair, and resolved to get the children lost once more, and to make sure of it by taking them much further away than the first time. But however much they tried to keep their plan a secret, Hop o' my Thumb still heard them talking about it. He counted on being able to escape in the same way as before; but although he got up early so as to go and collect some little pebbles, he did not succeed, because he found that the door of the house had been double-locked. He could not think what to do, until the woodcutter's wife gave them each a piece of bread for their breakfast, when it occurred to him that he could use breadcrumbs instead of pebbles, if he dropped them behind him along the paths where they would be going, and he put the bread away in his pocket.

Their father and mother led them into the thickest and darkest part of the forest, and as soon as they reached it they slipped away secretly along a side path, and left the children there. Hop o' my Thumb was not too worried, since he believed that he could easily find his way by following the trail of breadcrumbs that he had dropped wherever they had passed; but he had a nasty surprise when he could not find a single crumb; the birds had come and eaten them all. So the children were very miserable; the further they walked the more they got lost, and the deeper they went into the forest. Night fell, and a great wind began blowing, which frightened them dreadfully. On every side they thought they could hear the noise of wolves howling, and coming closer to eat them. They hardly dared talk to each other or look round. It started to rain heavily, and they got soaked to the skin. At every step they slipped and fell into the mud, so that when they got up they were all dirty, not knowing how to get their hands clean.

Hop o' my Thumb climbed up into a tree to see if he could make anything out. He looked around in every direction and saw a faint light which looked like a candle, but it was a long way off, outside the forest. He came down from the tree, and when he was on the ground he could no longer see anything. This alarmed him, but when he and his brothers had walked for some time towards the light he had seen, he saw it again as they came out from the wood. At last they reached the house where the candle was, but not without many a scare before they got there, because they had often lost sight of it, which happened whenever their path took them into a dip in the ground.

They knocked on the door and the housewife came to open it. She asked what they wanted; Hop o' my Thumb said that they were poor children who had got lost in the forest, and asked her if she would let them sleep there, out of charity. Seeing what fine boys they were the woman started to cry, saying: "Alas! my poor lads, what have you done by coming here? Didn't you know that this house belongs to an ogre who eats little children?"

"Alas!" answered Hop o' my Thumb, trembling all over, like his brothers, "what shall we do? The wolves in the forest are bound to eat us tonight, if you will not give us shelter in your house. And in that case we would prefer the gentleman here to eat us; perhaps he will have pity on us if you would be kind enough to ask him."

The Ogre's wife, thinking that she could keep them hidden from her husband until the next morning, let them come in, and took them to get warm in front of a blazing fire; for there was a whole sheep roasting on the spit for the Ogre's supper. As they were beginning to get warm, they heard someone knocking loudly on the door three or four times; it was the Ogre coming back. His wife immediately hid them under the bed, and went to open the door. The first thing the Ogre did was to ask whether his supper was ready and whether his wine had been drawn for him; then he at once sat down to table. The sheep was still red with blood, but to him it seemed all the better for it. He sniffed to right and left, saying that he could smell fresh meat. "It must be that calf which I have dressed ready for cutting up that you can smell," said his wife.

"I can smell fresh meat, as I've told you already," retorted the Ogre, looking crossly at his wife, "and there's something going on here that I don't know about." And as he spoke he got up from the table and went straight over to the bed. "Aha!" he said, "so you have been playing tricks on me, have you! A curse on you, woman! I don't know why I don't eat you too; it's lucky for you that you're old and tough. But here's some game that will do nicely for three of my Ogre friends who should be coming to see me some day soon."

He pulled them out from under the bed one after the other. The poor children knelt down and begged for mercy, but the Ogre they had to deal with was the cruellest ogre of all, and far from taking pity on them he was already devouring them with his eyes, telling his wife that they would be tasty morsels when she had made a good sauce to go with them. He went to fetch a carving knife, and went across to the wretched children, sharpening it as he did so on a long whetstone which he held in his left hand. He had already taken hold of one of the boys when his wife said: "What are you doing, at this hour of the night? Isn't there time enough tomorrow morning?"

"Quiet," replied the Ogre, "the meat will taste better if it hangs longer."

"You've already got plenty of meat hanging up," his wife answered; "there's a calf, two sheep, and half a pig!"

"You're right," said the Ogre; "give them a good supper, so that they won't get thin, and put them to bed." The good woman was delighted, and brought them some supper, but they were too frightened to eat anything. As for the Ogre, he went back to his wine delighted to have such a good treat for his friends, and drank twice as much as usual, which went to his head and made him go off to bed.

The Ogre had seven daughters, who were still children. These little ogresses had very fine complexions, because they ate fresh meat like their father, but they had small eyes, very round and grey, hooked noses, and very big mouths that had long sharp teeth with wide gaps in between. They were not yet really wicked, but showed great promise; already they would bite little children to suck their blood. They had been taken up to bed early, and all seven of them were lying in a wide bed, with golden crowns on their heads. Another bed just as wide was in the same room, and in this one the Ogre's wife put the seven little boys for the night, after which she went to bed next to her husband.

Hop o' my Thumb, who had noticed that the Ogre's daughters had golden crowns on their heads, was afraid that the Ogre would feel remorse for not cutting the boys' throats that same night, so he got up in the middle of the night and, taking the caps that he and his brothers were wearing, he put them very gently on the heads of the Ogre's daughters, first removing their golden crowns, which he put on his own and his brothers' heads, so that the Ogre might mistake them for his daughters, and his daughters for the boys whose throats he meant to cut.

It happened just as he thought; for the Ogre, waking up about midnight, was sorry that he had delayed until next day the business that he could have done the day before. He jumped quickly out of bed and took his carving knife, saying: "Let's just see how my fine little lads are keeping; we'll get it over and done with this time." He groped his way up to his daughters' bedroom in the dark and went to the bed where the little boys were; they were all asleep, except for Hop o' my Thumb, who was scared out of his wits when he felt the Ogre's hand on his head, after he had tried the other brothers' heads already. Having felt the golden crowns, the Ogre said to himself: "My word! I'd have made a fine mess of things there. Obviously I drank too much last night."

Then he went to his daughters' bed, where he could feel the caps belonging to the little boys. "Aha! there they are," he said, "the fine fellows! let's get to work." And with these words he set to without hesitation and cut the throats of all his seven daughters. And very pleased with himself for having settled the matter so quickly, he went back to bed beside his wife. As soon as Hop o' my Thumb heard the Ogre snoring, he woke his brothers and told them to get dressed and follow him. They went quietly down to the garden and jumped over the wall. They ran almost all night, trembling all the time, and not knowing where they were going.

When the Ogre woke up, he told his wife: "Go upstairs and dress those lads from last night." The Ogress was very surprised by such kindness from her husband, not suspecting that he meant her to get them ready for cutting up; she thought that he was telling her to put their clothes on. She went upstairs, and was completely taken by surprise to see her seven daughters with their throats cut and bathed in blood. The first thing she did was to faint (which is what almost all women resort to first in such circumstances). The Ogre, fearing that his wife would take too long over the task, went up to help, and was just as amazed as she had been when he saw the dreadful spectacle before him. "Ah! what have I done?" he cried. "The little wretches! – I'll soon pay them back for this." He threw a jugful of water in his wife's face, and when she had recovered her senses he said: "Give me my seven-league boots so that I can go and catch them."

He set off to track them down, and when he had run great distances in every direction, he finally came upon the children's trail; they were no more than a stone's throw from their father's house. They could see the Ogre stepping from mountain to mountain; he crossed rivers as easily as if they were tiny streams. Hop o' my Thumb, seeing a hollow in a rock nearby, made his brothers hide in it, and squeezed in after them, watching all the time to see what had become of the Ogre.

The Ogre, who was very weary after having travelled all that way to no purpose (for seven-league boots are tiring for the person who wears them), decided to have a rest; by chance, he came to sit down on the rock where the boys were hiding. He was so exhausted that he could go no further, and after he had rested for a while he went to sleep, and began to snore so dreadfully that the poor children were just as frightened as when he had had his carving knife in his hand to cut their throats. Hop o' my Thumb was not as frightened, and told his brothers that they must escape quickly and run into their house while the Ogre was fast asleep, and that they were not to worry about him. They did as he suggested and soon reached the house.

Hop o' my Thumb went up to the Ogre and gently pulled his boots off; then he put them on himself. They were very big and very wide, but they were magic boots, and had the power of becoming larger or smaller to suit the legs of whoever put them on, so that they fitted Hop o' my Thumb as closely as if they had been made for him. He went straight back to the Ogre's house, where he found the wife in tears beside her daughters who had had their throats cut.

"Your husband is in great danger," Hop o' my Thumb told her; "for he has been captured by a gang of robbers, who have sworn to kill him unless he gives them all his gold and silver. Just when they were holding a knife to his throat, he saw me, and

begged me to come and tell you of the danger he is in, and say that you are to give me everything he owns that is of value, and not to keep anything back, because otherwise they will kill him without mercy. The message was so urgent that he told me to take his seven-league boots, as you can see, so as to make haste, and also so that you will not think that I am an impostor." The good woman was very alarmed and immediately gave him everything she had, for the Ogre was a very good husband to her, even though he ate small children. So Hop o' my Thumb, laden with all the Ogre's wealth, went back to his father's house, where he was welcomed with great rejoicing.

Now there are many people who disagree about this last incident, and who claim that Hop o' my Thumb never stole the Ogre's money, although they admit that he had no scruples about taking his seven-league boots, because all they were ever used for was to chase small children. These people declare that their information comes from a reliable witness, since they have in fact been given food and drink in the woodcutter's house. They affirm that, when Hop o' my Thumb put the Ogre's boots on, he went to the King's court, knowing that they were very anxious there about an army that was two hundred leagues away, and wanted to know the outcome of a battle that had been fought. They say that he went to see the King, and told him that if he wished he would bring him news of the army before the day was out. The King promised him a large sum of money if he was successful. Hop o' my Thumb brought the news that very evening, and having made himself well known by this first commission, he was able to earn as much as he wanted, for the King paid him handsomely to carry his commands to the army, and innumerable ladies gave him whatever he wanted in order to get news of their lovers, which brought him more money than anything else. There were some women who entrusted him with letters for their husbands, but they paid him so badly, and it amounted to so little, that he never bothered to count what he had earned in this way.

After he had been in business as a courier for a time, and had amassed great wealth, he went back home to his father's house, where the rapturous welcome he received is beyond all imagining. He gave all his family enough for them to live in comfort, and established his father and brothers in official posts that had just been created; in this way he started them all on their careers, while improving his own position at Court in the best possible manner.

The Moral of this Tale

If every son grows strong and tall,
Well-mannered and well-liked by all,
Then parents with large families are pleased;
But when a son is silent, weak, and small,
He's likely to be bullied, mocked, and teased.
But sometimes it's the smallest who does best,
And brings prosperity to all the rest.

CHARLES PERRAULT lived in France during the reign of Louis XIV – called the Sun King – and while the royal family and the nobles lived in great prosperity, the rest of the country was suffering from famine. Hop o' my Thumb's courage and resilience has inspired generations of French children who have asked to hear this bedtime story again and again.

The Twelve
Dancing
Princesses

THE BROTHERS GRIMM

THERE WAS A KING WHO HAD TWELVE BEAUTIFUL daughters. They slept in twelve beds all in one room; and when they went to bed, the doors were shut and locked up; but every morning their shoes were found to be quite worn through as if they had been danced in all night; and yet nobody could find out how it happened, or where they had been.

Then the King made it known to all the land, that if any person could discover the secret, and find out where it was that the princesses danced in the night, he should have the one he liked best for his wife, and should be king after his death; but whoever tried and did not succeed, after three days and nights, should be put to death.

A king's son soon came. He was well entertained, and in the evening was taken to the chamber next to the one where the princesses lay in their twelve beds. There he was to sit and watch where they went to dance; and, in order that nothing might pass without his hearing it, the door of his chamber was left open. But the king's son soon fell asleep; and when he awoke in the morning he found that the princesses had all been dancing, for the soles of their shoes were full of holes. The same thing happened the second and third night: so the King ordered his head to be cut off. After him came several others; but they had all the same luck, and all lost their lives in the same manner.

Now it chanced that an old soldier, who had been wounded in battle and could fight no longer, passed through the country where this king reigned: and as he was travelling through a wood, he met an old woman, who asked him where he was going. "I hardly know where I am going, or what I had better do," said the soldier; "but I think I should like very well to find out where it is that the princesses dance, and then in time I might be a king." "Well," said the old dame, "that is no very hard task: only take care not to drink any of the wine which one of the princesses will bring to you in the evening; and as soon as she leaves you pretend to be fast asleep."

Then she gave him a cloak, and said, "As soon as you put that on you will become invisible, and you

will then be able to follow the princesses wherever they go." When the soldier heard all this good counsel, he determined to try his luck: so he went to the King, and said he was willing to undertake the task.

He was as well received as the others had been, and the King ordered fine royal robes to be given him; and when the evening came he was led to the outer chamber. Just as he was going to lie down, the eldest of the princesses brought him a cup of wine; but the soldier threw it all away secretly, taking care not to drink a drop. Then he laid himself down on his bed, and in a little while began to snore very loud as if he was fast asleep. When the twelve princesses heard this they laughed heartily; and the eldest said, "This fellow too might have done a wiser thing than lose his life in this way!" Then they rose up and opened their drawers and boxes, and took out all their fine clothes, and dressed themselves at the glass, and skipped about as if they were eager to begin dancing. But the youngest said, "I don't know how it is, while you are so happy I feel very uneasy; I am sure some mischance will befall us." "You simpleton," said the eldest, "you are always afraid; have you forgotten how many kings' sons have already watched in vain? And as for this soldier, even if I had not give him his sleeping draught, he would have slept soundly enough."

When they were all ready, they went and looked at the soldier; but he snored on, and did not stir hand or foot: so they thought they were quite safe; and the eldest went up to her own bed and clapped her hands, and the bed sunk into the floor and a trapdoor flew open. The soldier saw them going down through the trapdoor one after another, the eldest leading the way; and thinking he had no time to lose, he jumped up, put on the cloak which the old woman had given him, and followed them; but in the middle of the stairs he trod on the gown of the youngest princess, and she cried out to her sisters, "All is not right; someone took hold of my gown." "You silly creature!" said the eldest, "it is nothing but a nail in the wall." Then down they all went, and at the bottom they found themselves in a most delightful grove of trees; and the leaves were all of silver, and glittered and sparkled beautifully. The soldier wished to take away some token of the place; so he broke off a little branch, and there came a loud noise from the tree. Then the youngest daughter said again, "I am sure all is not right – did not you hear that noise? That never happened before." But the eldest said, "It is only our princes, who are shouting for joy at our approach."

Then they came to another grove of trees, where all the leaves were of gold; and afterwards to a third, where the leaves were all glittering diamonds. And the soldier broke a branch from each; and every time there was a loud noise, which made the youngest sister tremble with fear; but the eldest still said, it was only the princes, who were crying for joy. So they went on till they came to a great lake; and at the side of the lake there lay twelve little boats with twelve handsome princes in them, who seemed to be waiting there for the princesses.

One of the princesses went into each boat, and the soldier stepped into the same boat with the youngest. As they were rowing over the lake, the prince who was in the boat with the youngest princess and the soldier said, "I do not know why it is, but though I am rowing with all my might we do not get on so fast as usual, and I am quite tired: the boat seems very heavy today." "It is only the heat of the weather," said the princess: "I feel it very warm too."

On the other side of the lake stood a fine illu-
minated castle, from which came the merry music
of horns and trumpets. There they all landed, and
went into the castle, and each prince danced with
his princess; and the soldier, who was all the time
invisible, danced with them too; and when any of the
princesses had a cup of wine set by her, he drank it
all up, so that when she put the cup to her mouth it
was empty. At this, too, the youngest sister was terribly frightened, but the eldest always silenced her.
They danced on till three o'clock in the morning,
and then all their shoes were worn out, so that they
were obliged to leave off. The princes rowed them
back again over the lake (but this time the soldier
placed himself in the boat with the eldest princess);
and on the opposite shore they took leave of each
other, the princesses promising to come again the
next night.

When they came to the stairs, the soldier ran on
before the princesses, and laid himself down; and as
the twelve sisters slowly came up very much tired,
they heard him snoring in his bed; so they said, "Now
all is quite safe"; then they undressed themselves, put
away their fine clothes, pulled off their shoes, and

went to bed. In the morning the soldier said nothing about what had happened, but determined to see more of this strange adventure, and went again the second and third night; and everything happened just as before; the princesses danced each time till their shoes were worn to pieces, and then returned home. However, on the third night the soldier carried away one of the golden cups as a token of where he had been.

As soon as the time came when he was to declare the secret, he was taken before the King with the three branches and the golden cup; and the twelve princesses stood listening behind the door to hear what he would say. And when the King asked him, "Where do my twelve daughters dance at night?" he answered, "With twelve princes in a castle under ground." And then he told the King all that had happened, and showed him the three branches and the golden cup which he had brought with him. Then the King called for the princesses, and asked them whether what the soldier said was true: and when they saw that they were discovered, and that it was of no use to deny what had happened, they confessed it all. And the King asked the soldier which of them he would choose for his wife; and he answered, "I am not very young, so I will have the eldest." – And they were married that very day, and the soldier was chosen to be the King's heir.

THE BROTHERS GRIMM (Jacob and Wilhelm) were born in Germany in 1785 and 1786 respectively. They were very close, and collected and wrote more than 200 fairy tales and folktales in the early 1800s. It is because of them that we know stories such as 'Rapunzel', 'Hansel and Gretel' and 'Snow White'.

The
Red Shoes

HANS CHRISTIAN ANDERSEN

THERE WAS ONCE A LITTLE GIRL, VERY NICE AND very pretty, but so poor that she had to go barefooted all summer. And in winter she had to wear thick wooden shoes that chafed her ankles until they were red, oh, as red as could be.

In the middle of the village lived Old Mother Shoemaker. She took some old scraps of red cloth and did her best to make them into a little pair of shoes. They were a bit clumsy, but well meant, for she intended to give them to the little girl. Karen was the little girl's name.

The first time Karen wore her new red shoes was on the very day when her mother was buried. Of course, they were not right for mourning, but they were all she had, so she put them on and walked barelegged after the plain wicker coffin.

Just then a large old carriage came by, with a large old lady inside it. She looked at the little girl and took pity upon her. And she went to the parson

and said: "Give the little girl to me, and I shall take good care of her."

Karen was sure that this happened because she wore red shoes, but the old lady said the shoes were hideous, and ordered them burned. Karen was given proper new clothes. She was taught to read, and she was taught to sew. People said she was pretty, but her mirror told her, "You are more than pretty. You are beautiful."

It happened that the Queen came travelling through the country with her little daughter, who was a princess. Karen went with all the people who flocked to see them at the castle. The little princess, all dressed in white, came to the window to let them admire her. She didn't wear a train, and she didn't wear a gold crown, but she did wear a pair of splendid red morocco shoes. Of course, they were much nicer than the ones Old Mother Shoemaker had put together for little Karen, but there's nothing in the world like a pair of red shoes!

When Karen was old enough to be confirmed, new clothes were made for her, and she was to have new shoes. They went to the house of a thriving shoemaker, to have him take the measure of her little feet.

In his shop were big glass cases, filled with the prettiest shoes and the shiniest boots. They looked most attractive but, as the old lady did not see very well, they did not attract her. Among the shoes there was a pair of red leather ones which were just like those the Princess had worn. How perfect they were! The shoemaker said he had made them for the daughter of a count, but that they did not quite fit her.

"They must be patent leather to shine so," said the old lady.

"Yes, indeed they shine," said Karen. As the shoes fitted Karen, the old lady bought them, but she had no idea they were red. If she had known that, she would never have let Karen wear them to confirmation, which is just what Karen did.

Every eye was turned towards her feet. When she walked up the aisle to the chancel of the church, it seemed to her as if even those portraits of bygone ministers and their wives, in starched ruffs and long black gowns – even they fixed their eyes upon her red shoes. She could think of nothing else, even when the pastor laid his hands upon her head and spoke of her holy baptism, and her covenant with God, and her duty as a Christian. The solemn organ rolled, the children sang sweetly, and the old choir leader sang too, but Karen thought of nothing except her red shoes.

Before the afternoon was over, the old lady had heard from everyone in the parish that the shoes were red. She told Karen it was naughty to wear red shoes to church. Highly improper! In the future she was always to wear black shoes to church, even though they were her old ones.

Next Sunday there was holy communion. Karen looked at her black shoes. She looked at her red ones. She kept looking at her red ones until she put them on.

It was a fair, sunny day. Karen and the old lady took the path through the cornfield, where it was rather dusty. At the church door they met an old soldier, who stood with a crutch and wore a long, curious beard. It was more reddish than white. In fact it was quite red. He bowed down to the ground, and asked the old lady if he might dust her shoes. Karen put out her little foot too.

"Oh, what beautiful shoes for dancing," the soldier said. "Never come off when you dance," he told the shoes, as he tapped the sole of each of them with his hand.

The old lady gave the soldier a penny, and went on into the church with Karen. All the people there stared at Karen's red shoes, and all the portraits stared too. When Karen knelt at the altar rail, and even when the chalice came to her lips, she could think only of her red shoes. It was as if they kept floating around in the chalice, and she forgot to sing the psalm. She forgot to say the Lord's Prayer.

Then church was over, and the old lady got into her carriage. Karen was lifting her foot to step in after her when the old soldier said, "Oh, what beautiful shoes for dancing!"

Karen couldn't resist taking a few dancing steps, and once she began her feet kept on dancing. It was as if the shoes controlled her. She danced round the corner of the church – she simply could not help it. The coachman had to run after her, catch her, and lift her into the carriage. But even there her feet went on dancing so that she gave the good old lady a terrible kicking. Only when she took her shoes off did her legs quiet down. When they got home the shoes were put away in a cupboard, but Karen would still go and look at them.

Shortly afterwards the old lady was taken ill, and it was said she could not recover. She required constant care and faithful nursing, and for this she depended on Karen. But a great ball was being given in the town, and Karen was invited. She looked at the old lady, who could not live in any case. She looked at the red shoes, for she thought there was no harm in looking. She put them on, for she thought there was no harm in that either. But then she went to the ball and began dancing. When she tried to turn to the right, the shoes turned to the left. When she wanted to dance up the ballroom, her shoes danced down. They danced down the stairs, into the street, and out through the gate of the town. Dance she did, and dance she must, straight into the dark woods.

Suddenly something shone through the trees, and she thought it was the moon, but it turned out to be the red-bearded soldier. He nodded and said, "Oh, what beautiful shoes for dancing."

She was terribly frightened, and tried to take off her shoes. She tore off her stockings, but the shoes had grown fast to her feet. And dance she did, for dance she must, over fields and valleys, in the rain and in the sun, by day and night. It was most dreadful by

73

night. She danced over an unfenced graveyard, but the dead did not join her dance. They had better things to do. She tried to sit on a pauper's grave, where the bitter fennel grew, but there was no rest or peace for her there. And when she danced towards the open doors of the church, she saw it guarded by an angel with long white robes and wings that reached from his shoulders down to the ground. His face was grave and stern, and in his hand he held a broad, shining sword.

"Dance you shall!" he told her. "Dance in your red shoes until you are pale and cold, and your flesh shrivels down to the skeleton. Dance you shall from door to door, and wherever there are children proud and vain you must knock at the door till they hear you, and are afraid of you. Dance you shall. Dance always."

"Have mercy upon me!" screamed Karen. But she did not hear the angel answer. Her shoes swept her out through the gate, and across the fields, along highways and byways, forever and always dancing.

One morning she danced by a door she knew well. There was the sound of a hymn, and a coffin was carried out covered with flowers. Then she knew the old lady was dead. She was all alone in the world now, and cursed by the angel of God.

Dance she did and dance she must, through the dark night. Her shoes took her through thorn and briar that scratched her until she bled. She danced across the wastelands until she came to a lonely little house. She knew that this was where the executioner lived, and she tapped with her finger on his window pane.

"Come out!" she called. "Come out! I can't come in, for I am dancing."

The executioner said, "You don't seem to know who I am. I strike off the heads of bad people, and I feel my axe beginning to quiver."

"Don't strike off my head, for then I could not repent of my sins," said Karen. "But strike off my feet with the red shoes on them."

She confessed her sin, and the executioner struck off her feet with the red shoes on them. The shoes danced away with her little feet, over the fields into the deep forest. But he made wooden feet and a pair of crutches for her. He taught her a hymn that prisoners sing when they are sorry for what they have done. She kissed his hand that held the axe, and went back across the wasteland.

"Now I have suffered enough for those red shoes," she said. "I shall go and be seen again in the church." She hobbled to church as fast as she could, but when she got there the red shoes danced in front of her, and she was frightened and turned back.

All week long she was sorry, and cried many bitter tears. But when Sunday came again she said, "Now I have suffered and cried enough. I think I must be as good as many who sit in church and hold their heads high." She started out unafraid, but the moment she came to the church gate she saw her red shoes dancing before her. More frightened than ever, she turned away, and with all her heart she really repented.

She went to the pastor's house, and begged him to give her work as a servant. She promised to work hard, and do all that she could. Wages did not matter, if only she could have a roof over her head and be with good people. The pastor's wife took pity on her, and gave her work at the parsonage. Karen was faithful and serious. She sat quietly in the evening, and listened to every word when the pastor read the Bible aloud. The children were devoted to her, but when they spoke of frills and furbelows, and of being as beautiful as a queen, she would shake her head.

When they went to church next Sunday they asked her to go too, but with tears in her eyes she looked at her crutches, and shook her head. The others went to hear the word of God, but she went to her lonely little room, which was just big enough to hold her bed and one chair. She sat with her hymnal in her hands, and as she read it with a contrite heart she heard the organ roll. The wind carried the sound from the church to her window. Her face was wet with tears as she lifted it up, and said, "Help me, O Lord!"

Then the sun shone bright, and the white-robed angel stood before her. He was the same angel she had seen that night, at the door of the church. But he no longer held a sharp sword. In his hand was a green branch, covered with roses. He touched the ceiling with it. There was a golden star where it touched, and the ceiling rose high. He touched the walls and they opened wide. She saw the deep-toned organ. She saw the portraits of ministers and their wives. She saw the congregation sit in flower-decked pews, and sing from their hymnals. Either the church had come to the poor girl in her narrow little room, or it was she who had been brought to the church. She sat in the pew with the pastor's family. When they had finished the hymn, they looked up and nodded to her.

"It was right for you to come, little Karen," they said.

"It was God's own mercy," she told them.

The organ sounded and the children in the choir sang, softly and beautifully. Clear sunlight streamed warm through the window, right down to the pew where Karen sat. She was so filled with the light of it, and with joy and with peace, that her heart broke. Her soul travelled along the shaft of sunlight to heaven, where no one questioned her about the red shoes.

HANS CHRISTIAN ANDERSEN wrote this story in 1845. He was the Danish son of a shoemaker, who died when he was 12. His fairy tales are famous all around the world.

The Story of
Chernushka

ALEXANDER
NIKOLAYEVICH
AFANASYEV

ONCE UPON A TIME THERE LIVED A GENTLEMAN who had a kind wife and a beautiful daughter called Masha. But his wife died, and soon after he married a widow. She had two daughters of her own, and they were mean and spiteful girls! They both bullied poor Masha. They forced her to do their chores for them, and when there was no work to do they forced her to sit by the stove and rake out the cinders. Masha was always dirty and covered in soot, and so they called her Chernushka, which was the Russian for "Cinderella".

People started to say that the Prince wanted to get married, that he was planning to hold a big party where he would choose himself a wife. And indeed he was. The Prince invited everybody to his palace. Masha's stepmother and stepsisters started to get ready, but they refused to bring Masha; however much she begged, they wouldn't change their minds. So her stepmother and stepsisters set off for the Prince's party, and they left Masha with a whole sack of barley, flour and soot, all mixed up together. Her stepmother ordered her to separate all the grains from the soot by the time she got back.

Masha went out onto the doorstep and wept bitterly. Then two doves flew up, separated the barley, flour and soot for her, and alighted on her shoulders – and suddenly Masha was clothed in a splendid new gown. "Go to the party!" said the doves, "But be sure not to stay past midnight."

The moment Masha entered the palace, people began to stare at her in wonder. The Prince liked her most of all, and her stepmother and stepsisters didn't even recognize her. She enjoyed wandering through the party, and talking to the other girls there. Then she saw that it was nearly midnight; she remembered what the doves had said, and hastened home. The Prince hurried after her. He wanted to ask her who she was, but she was nowhere to be found.

The next day the Prince had another party. Masha's stepsisters bustled about, primping and preening, all the while screeching and swearing at Masha: "Oi, Chernushka! Dress us! Clean our clothes! Cook our dinner!" Masha obeyed, but when evening came, she had a wonderful time at the party and went home before midnight. The Prince hurried after her – but again she got away.

On the third day, the Prince provided a lavish banquet. That evening, the doves shod and clothed Masha even better than before. She went into the palace, and enjoyed the party so much that she forgot all about the time. All of a sudden it struck midnight; Masha quickly ran home, but the Prince had ordered the whole staircase to be spread with pitch and tar. One of her slippers stuck to the pitch and stayed on the staircase. The Prince picked it up and the very next day he ordered his men to find the girl whose foot fitted the slipper.

They scoured the whole town – but the slipper wouldn't fit on anyone's foot. At last they came to Masha's house. Her stepmother tried to squeeze the elder daughter's foot into the slipper – but no, it didn't fit, her foot was too big! "Chop off your big toe!" the stepmother said to her daughter. "When you're a princess you won't need to do any walking!" So she chopped off her toe and put on the slipper. The Prince's messengers started leading her off to the palace, but then the doves flew up and started to coo: "Look – there's blood on her foot! Look – there's

blood on her foot!" The messengers had a look and saw blood flowing from the girl's slipper. "You're right," they said, "It doesn't fit!" The stepmother tried the slipper on her other daughter, and the same thing happened with her.

Then the messengers saw Masha and ordered her to try it on. She put the slipper on her foot – and suddenly she was clothed in a beautiful, shining gown. Her stepsisters were awestruck! Masha was taken to the Prince's palace, and the next day they were married. When she and the Prince approached the altar, the two doves flew up and alighted one on each of her shoulders. When the newlyweds came back from the church, the doves swooped down and pecked out an eye from each of Masha's stepsisters.

The wedding was a very merry affair. I was there. We drank honey beer and it spilt on my moustache and didn't go into my mouth.

ALEXANDER NIKOLAYEVICH AFANASYEV was an outstanding collector of Russian folktales. He was born in 1826 in the Voronezh region of Russia, and went on to publish nearly 600 fairy tales and folktales, many of which inspired later writers and composers.

Brer Rabbit
and Mr. Dog

JOEL CHANDLER HARRIS

"DEY WUZ ONE TIME W'EN OLE BRER RABBIT 'UZ bleedzd ter go ter town atter sump'n n'er fer his fambly, an' he mos' 'shame' ter go kaze his shoes done wo' teetotally out. Yit he bleedzd ter go, an' he put des ez good face on it ez he kin, an' he take down he walkin'-cane an' sot out des ez big ez de next un.

"Well, den, ole Brer Rabbit go on down de big road twel he come ter de place whar some folks bin camp out de night befo', an' he sot down by de fier, he did, fer ter worn his foots, kaze dem mawnin's 'uz sorter col', like deze yer mawnin's. He sot dar an' look at his toes, an' he feel mighty sorry fer hisse'f.

"Well, den, he sot dar, he did, en 'twa'n't long 'fo' he year sump'n n'er trottin' down de road, an' he tuck'n look up an' yer come Mr. Dog a-smellin' an' a-snuffin' 'roun' fer ter see ef de folks lef' any scraps by der camp-fier. Mr. Dog 'uz all dress up in his Sunday-go-ter-meetin' cloze, an' mo'n dat, he had on a pa'r er bran' new shoes.

"Well, den, w'en Brer Rabbit see dem ar shoes he feel mighty bad, but he ain't let on. He bow ter Mr. Dog mighty perlite, an' Mr. Dog he bow back, he did, an' dey pass de time er day, kaze dey 'uz ole 'quaintance. Brer Rabbit, he say:

"'Mr. Dog, whar you gwine all fix up like dis?'

"'I gwine ter town, Brer Rabbit; whar you gwine?'

"'I thought I go ter town myse'f fer ter git me new pa'r shoes, kaze my ole uns done wo' out en dey hu'ts my foots so bad I can't w'ar um. Dem mighty nice shoes w'at you got on, Mr. Dog; whar you git um?'

"'Down in town, Brer Rabbit, down in town.'

"'Dey fits you mighty slick, Mr. Dog, an' I wish you be so good ez ter lemme try one un um on.'

"Brer Rabbit talk so mighty sweet dat Mr. Dog sot right flat on de groun' an' tuck off one er de behime shoes, an' loan't it ter Brer Rabbit. Brer Rabbit, he lope off down de road en den he come back. He tell Mr. Dog dat de shoe fit mighty nice, but wid des one un um on, hit make 'im trot crank-sided.

"Well, den, Mr. Dog, he pull off de yuther behime shoe, an' Brer Rabbit trot off an' try it. He come back, he did, an' he say:

"'Dey mighty nice, Mr. Dog, but dey sorter r'ars me up behime, an' I dunner zackly how dey feels.'

"Dis make Mr. Dog feel like he wanter be perlite, an' he take off de befo' shoes, an' Brer Rabbit put um on an' stomp his foots, an 'low:

"'Now dat sorter feel like shoes;' an' he rack off down de road, an' w'en he git whar he oughter tu'n 'roun', he des lay back he years an' keep on gwine; an' 'twa'n't long 'fo' he git outer sight.

"Mr. Dog, he holler, an' tell 'im fer ter come back, but Brer Rabbit keep on gwine; Mr. Dog, he holler, Mr. Rabbit, he keep on gwine. An' down ter dis day," continued 'Tildy, smacking her lips, and showing her white teeth, "Mr. Dog bin a-runnin' Brer Rabbit, an' ef you'll des go out in de woods wid any Dog on dis place, des time he smell de Rabbit track he'll holler an' tell 'im fer ter come back."

"Dat's de Lord's trufe!" said Aunt Tempy.

JOEL CHANDLER HARRIS was an American journalist and folklorist from Georgia. His first collection of folktales based on the African-American oral storytelling tradition was published in 1880. It was an instant success, and his stories – among which the most famous are the 'Brer Rabbit' tales – inspired generations of writers.

Perseus and the Winged Sandals

MURIELLE SZAC

THE YEARS HAVE PASSED, PERSEUS HAS GROWN.
He has become a handsome young man, strong
and brave. On this island, however, where he had
been so warmly welcomed, an enemy is lying in
wait for him. The king of the island has fallen in
love with his mother, the beautiful Danae. This
king is a brute and Danae does not want to be his
wife. She refuses to marry him, claiming that she
must stay with her son to look after him. King
Polydectes, however, has no intention of giving up
on this marriage. So he decides to get rid of Perseus.
He invites him to dine at the palace, planning to
set a trap for him.

That evening, Perseus is among the first guests to
arrive at the palace. All the young men on the island
had been invited and they rejoiced in advance at the
idea of having a really good time. Perseus' good looks
did not pass unnoticed. The maidservants whispered
with admiration as he passed and the young man

noted this with pleasure. Because he really liked to please and to be noticed. The more the evening progressed, the more Perseus talked and laughed loud. The wine flowed in currents and he never ceased to drink, and to drink even more. Presiding at the banquet, at the centre of the table, the king did not take his eyes off Perseus. Soon, the king rose and asked for everyone's silence. "Dear friends," he began, "it is with great pleasure that I welcome each of you in my house. Amuse yourselves well! I would like to thank all those of you who have brought me gifts. You, Lycos, for this magnificent black horse which is pawing the ground outside my door. You, Nepumenus, for this splendid grey mare. And you, Aristos, for this golden-eyed colt, which shall be the pride of my stables." The king addressed himself in turn to all the guests present around the table. Most of them, knowing his passion for horses, had offered him a new one.

The others had brought him gems or precious objects. As he heard the list of gifts, Perseus began to blush. He was too poor; he had come empty-handed. His turn was about to come and he felt crushed by shame. So as not to lose face, the proud young man leapt into the middle of the room before his name had even been pronounced. Wine and the thrill of the moment were making his head spin.

He shouted: "I, Perseus, the son of Danae, shall bring you the most extraordinary gift of all. I shall offer you the head of Medusa, the terrible Gorgon."

A murmur ran through the assembled guests. The Gorgons were three monstrous creatures who spread the reign of terror. These three repugnant sisters had, instead of hair, a multitude of serpents swarming on their heads. Above all, however, they transformed into stone any man who dared to look at them, even if it were only for an instant.

The king was delighted: his trap had worked. He had had strong hopes that Perseus, exasperated, would do something foolish. He said, smiling:

"Very well, my dear Perseus. Leave then at once and fetch me that Gorgon's head."

Perseus had made himself the centre of everyone's attention. Yet he had also just thrown himself into an adventure fraught with danger, for no one had ever come out alive from an encounter with the Gorgon.

Perseus went outside. The cold night wind lashed his face. Little by little he regained his spirits. His pride had made him throw himself right into the wolf's mouth. Without some help from the gods, he would never be able to pull through this one. He had been walking along the beach with his head bowed for quite some time, when someone laid a hand on his shoulder. It was Hermes, who had come to offer his assistance to his young protégé.

"I am Hermes, your half-brother," the god said to him.

"I could tell," replied Perseus, "there is no one else but you who wears a winged helmet and sandals."

They both sat on a rock. "I heard everything. Do you know where the Gorgons live?" asked Hermes.

Perseus shook his head mournfully: "Not even that!" he sighed.

"Well, in that case, you must first meet the Graeae. They are their sisters. They, and they alone, know where the Gorgons live. But be very careful, for they are as formidable themselves." As he leant over Perseus, Hermes really looked like an older brother advising the younger one. The moon was shedding a white light on them.

"You... will you come with me?" stammered Perseus, his voice hesitant all of a sudden. Nothing remained any more of the young braggart who had been boasting a few hours earlier in the king's palace.

Hermes smiled. He had not forgotten the laughter of the child shut up in the crate. "Yes," he replied, "I will accompany you."

They both decided to wait for dawn before setting out. They lay on the sand, huddling close to each other, and tried to get some rest.

❧

Perseus' meeting with Hermes had bolstered up his spirits, and he came to the mountain where the three Graeae lived feeling confident. The air was scalding hot and a cloud of dust rose at each step he took. The closer he approached, the more the landscape turned grey. The rays of the sun did not reach into this sinister region. The journey was long and painful. Yet each time he hesitated about which path to follow, Hermes would point him in the right direction. When he arrived at the cave of the three old women, he hid himself not too far from the entrance and waited. Soon he saw them appear. One could just barely make out their forms in the flickering light of a candle that one of them was carrying. They were horrible to look at. Their skin was yellow and wrinkled, like old crumpled paper. Their white hair fell in disarray over their shoulders, like skeins of string. And a foul smell exuded from their bodies, a smell of withered flowers and mustiness which stung one's throat.

"It is my turn to look! Pass me the eye!" said one of them in a harsh, metallic voice.

"No! It's my turn!" replied the other old woman, in an equally rasping tone.

"I am hungry, so give me the tooth!" cried the third sister.

Perseus then saw the one who had spoken first take out her solitary tooth and hand it to her sister. In the meantime, the second removed her solitary eye and passed it to the third sister. The three sisters shared a single eye and a single tooth among them. Perseus observed the three old women playing this game of pass the parcel; then he did as Hermes advised. As one of them was removing her eye to give it to one of the other two, he leapt forward and snatched the eye. The three Graeae could no longer see a thing! They began to shout and argue among themselves to find out which had taken the eye, but Perseus interrupted them and said in a strong voice: "It is I, Perseus, who holds your eye. If you wish me to give it back to you, show me the way that will lead me to your sisters the Gorgons." After a moment of bewilderment, the Graeae gave him all the directions he needed to reach the den where their horrible sisters were hiding. Perseus hesitated as to whether he ought to give them back the eye. Yet he had promised and he had to keep his word. He returned the eye to them and departed immediately.

Hermes had left him a little earlier and Perseus was now travelling alone.

"Well done, Perseus, continue like this, I am proud of you and I will help you too."

Who was speaking like this in Perseus' ear? Where did this congratulatory voice come from? Surprised, the young man stopped walking. He said rather nervously:

"But... But who are you? Show yourself!"

He heard a little laughter. Then a woman appeared on his path. She bore a helmet and a spear and she stood proudly erect in her armour. Perseus recognized immediately the goddess Athena.

"You are a brave young man," she said. "I know that my brother Hermes protects you but I would like to help you as well. After all, we all have the same father, don't we?" Intimidated by the great goddess, Perseus gave no answer. She approached him and held her shield out to him. "You know this already: any person who meets Medusa's gaze is transformed into stone. Take my shield. When you are in the presence of Medusa, turn the shield towards you, and use it as a mirror. You will be able to see her reflection on it. In this way, you can fight her without ever looking at her straight in the face."

Perseus took Athena's shield. It shone like the sun. When he lifted up his dazzled head to thank the goddess, she had already vanished...

Perseus was walking sure-footed towards the den of the three monsters, but Hermes did not feel so easy in his mind. That's why he had gone away: to seek help. Soon enough, he rejoined Perseus along the way, carrying a huge sack on his shoulder.

Hermes asked him: "Are you quite sure that you have everything you need in order to win?"

With the insouciance of his youth, Perseus answered: "Oh, well, we'll see when we get there!"

Hermes shook his head unhappily and sat on a rock. All of a sudden he, the spirited and impulsive young god, was feeling much more sensible than Perseus. "Perhaps as a result of learning more things and of discovering the world," he mulled, "I am becoming a little wiser?" He took the sack he had been carrying on his shoulder and threw it over to the young man. "Catch this bag, you might need it. You will find inside the helmet which makes one invisible, the one belonging to my uncle Hades, the king of the Underworld. I borrowed it from him. There is also a long and mighty sword, a sword so sturdy that even the Gorgons' thick, hard skin will not be able to withstand it. As for the sack itself, it is magical: it takes the form of whatever you slip inside it." Then he slowly took off his shoes and held out the winged sandals to Perseus. "I will lend these to you as well. You can return everything to me later."

This time, Perseus was properly armed to wage battle against the Gorgons. Happy as a child in front

of new toys, he put on the winged sandals, drew the long sword out of its scabbard, grabbed hold of Athena's shield and put on the helmet of Hades. He instantly became invisible and flew away towards the Gorgons' den. "Do not forget," Hermes cried after him, "you can only kill Medusa. She is the only one of the three Gorgons who can die, the other two are immortal, do not attack them!" Perseus, however, was already far away. Hermes' words were lost in the wind. The messenger god decided to follow the young man in order to keep an eye on him.

The Gorgons lived on an icy island battered by raging winds. Perseus flew first of all across the ocean, until he noticed an island with beautiful cold and deserted beaches. There he discovered an absolutely incredible landscape and he knew that he was approaching the Gorgons' lair. There were animals of every kind and some men as well. But as he approached, he realized that these were statues of stone. Each had met the gaze of one of the Gorgons and had been immediately transformed into a statue! Perseus landed and began to walk amidst the statues of stone. He was touched by the fate of all these wretched creatures and his anger rose up inside him.

When he reached the cave where the Gorgons lived, they were all three asleep. Perseus observed them on Athena's shield, which served him as a mirror. They were even more appalling than anything Perseus had been able to imagine. Their heads were aswarm with snakes writhing in every direction and their necks were covered with dragon scales. They had enormous golden wings and their hands bore talons of bronze. He flew above the sleeping Gorgons, yet his hand was reluctant to strike. If he missed his target, what would happen once the monstrous sisters were awake? And, what is more, which of the three was Medusa? Hermes again came to his aid. He indicated Medusa to him with a motion of his hand. Perseus then brandished his heavy sword while keeping a keen eye on Medusa in the mirror-shield.

And Athena, who was also watching discreetly from the heights of Olympus, guided his hand. His magic sword came crashing down and lopped off Medusa's head with one clean blow. He came down immediately, grabbed the head, catching hold of it by its vile snake-hair, and slipped it inside his sack without looking at it. He had thus escaped the terrible gaze which turned people into stone.

Instantly, an incredible winged horse emerged from Medusa's body, by the name of Pegasus. For a moment Perseus stood there dazzled, his breath taken away by the winged horse's beauty. He stretched out his hand towards the animal to catch it, but the horse immediately flew away towards Olympus and disappeared from Perseus' sight.

In the meantime, the other two Gorgons had woken up and were getting ready to go after Medusa's murderer. Would Perseus manage to escape his pursuers?

The winged sandals that Hermes had lent to Perseus were extraordinarily swift. And so he took flight. Behind him, the two Gorgons tore howling along. They screamed, spat, yelled with rage, threatened Perseus with a thousand cruel sufferings. But where had he gone? Perseus had just put back on the helmet that made him invisible. And soon enough they had to abandon their chase, for they couldn't see him anywhere. Perseus was wild with joy to have succeeded in such an exploit.

The day rose. Perseus came in sight of a black, rocky coast bounded by crystalline blue water. Suddenly a sun ray revealed to him an extraordinary sight. A naked young woman was chained to an enormous rock right by the sea. She was so beautiful, with her dark skin and its shimmering reflections, and her hair floating in the wind, that Perseus fell instantly in love with her. He drew nearer. She remained motionless and stared hard at the sea while silent tears ran down her cheeks.

"What are you doing here chained like this?" asked Perseus.

The young woman gave a little jump when she saw him appear. "I am called Andromeda and I am the only daughter of the king of Ethiopia," she murmured. "And I am waiting for the sea monster who is supposed to come and devour me."

Perseus could not believe his ears. "But what have you done to deserve such a horrid fate?" he exclaimed.

"I? Nothing!" Andromeda sighed. "But my mother is so proud of me that she declared everywhere that I was the most beautiful of all. She even dared say that I was more beautiful than the sea nymphs. The nymphs became vexed and asked Poseidon, the god of the Seas, to avenge them." Andromeda stopped speaking. She was staring hard at the horizon and Perseus followed her gaze. He saw something writhing on the sea surface. And this something was coming closer and closer. He felt the young girl shake like a leaf. "This is it! This is it!" she cried. "This horrid sea monster ravages everything in its passage. It makes my father's people suffer, devours the fishermen and their boats. And I must be sacrificed to it to placate its anger..."

The monster was just a few feet away from Andromeda. You could see its gaping mouth and its scaly skin. Its pointed tail thrashed the waves, splattering the sky with spume. Its enormous torso cut through the water like a ship sailing at full speed. Perseus unsheathed his magic sword and, with a kick of his winged sandals, landed on the monster's spine. Then he thrust his sword into the monster's shoulder. Surprised, the monster bucked. Yet Perseus did not lose his balance. Three times his sword came crashing down, and three times the sharp blade gashed the monster's neck. A torrent of blood was flowing out now, dyeing the sea red. The monster lowed; then, after having squirmed in every direction, it gave up the fight and let itself sink to the bottom of the sea. Perseus barely had time to withdraw his sword and fly away again. On the shore, a symphony of applause burst out. The country's inhabitants were arriving in all haste to hail the hero who had defeated the monster and rescued their princess. Among those enthusiastic spectators was also Hermes. He had watched his protégé with keen attention, ready to intervene if things went awry. But he was proud of Perseus: he had known how to manage on his own.

Perseus paid no attention to his public. He had hurried to Andromeda and with a stroke of his magic sword had severed the chains which held her prisoner. Andromeda's parents rushed forward and took her in their arms. But Andromeda pulled herself free and turned smiling towards Perseus. She opened her arms and the young man held her fast against his heart.

The Greek myths were tales of the gods, goddesses, heroes and heroines of ancient Greece. The stories are millennia old, and were passed down by word of mouth. MURIELLE SZAC is a French writer who has retold the Greek myths for children.

The Pair
of Shoes

PIERRE GRIPARI

THERE ONCE WAS A PAIR OF SHOES THAT GOT married. The right shoe, which was the man, was called Nicolas, and the left shoe, which was the lady, was called Tina.

They lived in a beautiful cardboard box where they lay wrapped in tissue paper. They were perfectly happy there, and they hoped things would go on like this for ever.

But then, one fine morning, a sales assistant took them out of their box so that a lady could try them on. The lady put them on, took a few steps, then, seeing that the shoes looked good on her, she said:

"I'll take them."

"Would you like the shoebox?" asked the sales assistant.

"No need," replied the lady, "I'll walk home in them."

She paid and left, her new shoes already on her feet.

So it was that Nicolas and Tina walked about for a whole day without a single glimpse of each other. Only that night were they reunited inside a dark cupboard.

"Is that you, Tina?"

"Yes, it's me, Nicolas."

"Ah, thank goodness! I thought you were lost!"

"Me too. But where were you?"

"Me? I was on the right foot."

"And I was on the left foot."

"Now I see it all," said Nicolas. "Every time you were in front, I was behind, and when you were behind, why, I was in front. That's why we couldn't see each other."

"And is this how it will be every day?" asked Tina.

"I'm afraid so!"

"But this is terrible! To spend all day without seeing you, my dear Nicolas! I shall never get used to this!"

"Listen," said Nicolas, "I have an idea. Since I am always on the right and you always on the left, well, every time I step forward, I shall make a little swerve towards you, at the same time. That way, we shall be able to say hello. All right?"

"All right!"

This, then, is what Nicolas did, in such a way that for the whole of the following day the lady wearing the shoes could not take three steps without her right foot bumping into her left heel, and every time it did – crash! She fell flat on the ground.

Very worried, that same day the lady went to consult a doctor.

"Doctor, I don't know what's wrong with me. I keep tripping myself up!"

"You trip yourself up?"

"Yes, doctor! Almost every time I take a step, my right foot catches my left heel and it makes me fall over!"

"This is very serious," said the doctor. "If it goes on, we shall have to cut off your right foot. But here is a prescription: this will get you ten thousand francs' worth of treatment. Pay me two thousand francs for the consultation, and come and see me tomorrow."

That evening, inside the cupboard, Tina asked Nicolas:

"Did you hear what the doctor said?"

"Yes, I heard."

"This is terrible! If they cut off the lady's right foot, she will throw you out, and we will be separated for ever! We must do something!"

"Yes, but what?"

"Listen, I have an idea: since I am on the left, tomorrow, I'll be the one who makes a little swerve to the right, every time I step forward! Okay?"

"Okay!"

Tina did as she said, so that on the second day, all day long it was the left foot that bumped into the right heel, and – crash! The poor lady found herself on the ground again. Even more worried, she went back to her doctor.

"Doctor, I am going from bad to worse! Now it's my left foot that is catching on my right heel!"

"This is even more serious," said the doctor. "If this goes on, we shall have to cut off both your feet! But wait, here is a prescription: this will get you a twenty-thousand-franc treatment. Give me three thousand francs for the consultation and, above all, don't forget to come back and see me tomorrow."

That evening, Nicolas asked Tina:

"Did you hear?"

"Yes, I heard."

"If they cut off both the lady's feet, what will become of us?"

"I can't bear to think of it!"

"I still love you, Tina!"

"Me too, Nicolas, I love you!"

"I want to be with you for ever!"

"Me too, that's what I want too!"

And so they talked, in the darkness, not suspecting that the lady who had bought them was pacing up and down in the corridor, in her slippers, because she couldn't get to sleep for thinking about the doctor's diagnosis. Walking past the cupboard door, she overheard the shoes' entire conversation and, being very intelligent, she understood everything.

"So that's what it is," she thought. "It isn't me who is ill, it's my shoes who are in love! How sweet!"

Upon which, she tossed the thirty thousand francs' worth of medicines that she had bought into the rubbish bin, and the following morning told her maid:

"Do you see that pair of shoes? I shan't wear them again, but I should like to keep them all the same. Now, polish them nicely, look after them, so that they are always shiny, and above all, never separate them from each other!"

As soon as she was alone, the maid said to herself:

"Madame is mad, to keep these shoes but never wear them! In a fortnight or so, when madame has forgotten all about it, I shall steal them!"

Two weeks later, she stole them and started wearing them. But as soon as she put them on, the cleaner too began to trip herself up. One evening, while she was on the back staircase taking the rubbish out, Nicolas and Tina tried to kiss, and *badaboom! Bang! Bump!* The cleaning lady came to rest on her behind on the landing, with a bird's-nest of potato peelings on her head and a strip of apple peel dangling in a spiral between her eyes, like a lock of hair.

"These shoes are witches," she thought. "I won't try wearing them again. I'll give them to my niece; she already has a limp!"

This is what she did. The niece, who did indeed have a limp, generally spent most of her days sitting in a chair, with her feet together. When she happened to go for a walk, she walked so slowly that she could hardly get her feet caught. And the shoes were

happy for, even during the day, they were mostly side by side.

This went on for a long time. Unfortunately, since the niece limped, she wore out one shoe faster than the other.

One evening, Tina said to Nicolas:

"I can feel that my sole is becoming thin, oh so thin! Very soon I shall have a hole!"

"Don't say that!" said Nicolas. "If they throw us out, we shall be separated again!"

"I know," said Tina, "but what can we do? I cannot help growing old!"

And so it happened: a week later, her sole had a hole in it. The limping niece bought a new pair of shoes and threw Nicolas and Tina into the rubbish bin.

"What will become of us?" worried Nicolas.

"I don't know," said Tina. "If only I could be sure of staying with you for ever!"

"Come close," said Nicolas, "and take my strap in yours. This way we shall not be parted."

So they did. Together they were tossed into the big bin; together they were taken away by the dustmen and left in a plot of wasteland. They stayed there together until the day when a little boy and a little girl found them.

"Oh, look at those shoes! They are arm in arm."

"That's because they're married," said the little girl.

"Well," said the little boy, "since they're married, they shall have a honeymoon!"

The little boy picked up the shoes, set them side by side on a plank, then carried the plank down to the water's edge and let it drift away, carried by the current, towards the sea. As the plank floated away, the little girl waved her handkerchief, calling:

"Goodbye, shoes, and have a wonderful journey!"

So it was that Nicolas and Tina, who were hoping for nothing more out of life, nevertheless had a beautiful honeymoon.

This story is originally part of a book of fairy tales written by PIERRE GRIPARI and published in 1967. They all take place in Paris, on rue Broca – a street that is hidden under a boulevard and where mysterious things happen. 'The Pair of Shoes' has been adapted for television numerous times... to the delight of children and grown-ups and alike!

About the Illustrator

LUCIE ARNOUX is a keen storyteller, who likes to spend a lot of time on her illustrations, and in her illustrations. She left her native south of France for London, because the grass there is genuinely greener – and they have tea. Since graduating from Kingston University in Illustration & Animation, she has settled in a cottage where she paints and doodles and enjoys life.

PUSHKIN CHILDREN'S BOOKS

Just as we all are, children are fascinated by stories. From the earliest age, we love to hear about monsters and heroes, romance and death, disaster and rescue, from every place and time.

We created Pushkin Children's Books to share these tales from different languages and cultures with younger readers, and to open the door to the wide, colourful worlds these stories offer.

From picture books and adventure stories to fairy tales and classics, and from fifty-year-old bestsellers to current huge successes abroad, the books on the Pushkin Children's list reflect the very best stories from around the world, for our most discerning readers of all: children.

THE WITCH IN THE BROOM CUPBOARD
AND OTHER TALES

PIERRE GRIPARI

Illustrated by Fernando Puig Rosado

'Wonderful... funny, tender and daft'
David Almond

THE STORY OF THE BLUE PLANET

ANDRI SNÆR MAGNASON

Illustrated by Áslaug Jónsdóttir

'A Seussian mix of wonder, wit and gravitas'
The New York Times

SHOLA AND THE LIONS

BERNARDO ATXAGA

Illustrated by Mikel Valverde

'Gently ironic stories... totally charming'
Independent

THE POINTLESS LEOPARD:
WHAT GOOD ARE KIDS ANYWAY?

COLAS GUTMAN

Illustrated by Delphine Perret

'Lively, idiomatic and always entertaining...
a decidedly offbeat little book'
Robert Dunbar, *Irish Times*

POCKETY: THE TORTOISE WHO LIVED AS SHE PLEASED

FLORENCE SEYVOS

Illustrated by Claude Ponti

'A treasure – a real find – and one of the most enjoyable children's books I've read in a while... This is a tortoise that deserves to win every literary race'
Observer

THE LETTER FOR THE KING

TONKE DRAGT

'Gripping from its opening moment onwards, this award-winning book doesn't miss a beat from its thrilling beginning to its satisfying ending'
Julia Eccleshare

THE PILOT AND THE LITTLE PRINCE

PETER SÍS

'With its extraordinary, sophisticated illustrations, its poetry and the historical detail of the text, this book will reward readers of any age over eight'
Sunday Times

SAVE THE STORY

GULLIVER · ANTIGONE · CAPTAIN NEMO · DON JUAN
GILGAMESH · THE BETROTHED · THE NOSE
CYRANO DE BERGERAC · KING LEAR · CRIME AND PUNISHMENT

'An amazing new series from Pushkin Press in which literary, adult authors retell classics (with terrific illustrations) for a younger generation'
Daily Telegraph

THE CAT WHO CAME IN OFF THE ROOF

ANNIE M.G. SCHMIDT

'Guaranteed to make anyone 7-plus to 107 who likes to
curl up with a book and a cat purr with pleasure'
The Times

THE OKSA POLLOCK SERIES

ANNE PLICHOTA AND CENDRINE WOLF

Part 1 · The Last Hope

Part 2 · The Forest of Lost Souls

Part 3 · The Heart of Two Worlds

'A feisty heroine, lots of sparky tricks and evil opponents
could fill a gap left by the end of the Harry Potter series'
Daily Mail

THE VITELLO SERIES

KIM FUPZ AAKESON

Illustrated by Niels Bo Bojesen

'Full of quirky humour and an anarchic sense
of fun that children will love'
Booktrust

A HOUSE WITHOUT MIRRORS

MÅRTEN SANDÉN

Illustrated by Moa Schulman

'A classic story that has it all'
Dagens Nyheter